Texas Twisters

Best wishes!
Anita Higman

by
Anita Higman

EAKIN PRESS 🔲 Austin, Texas

To
Moddy
(Ruth Kaul)

Thank you for your mothering,
your mentoring,
and the sweet melody
you love-cradled
into my
heart.

PLEASE TAKE NOTE:

Efforts have been made to offer current tornadic safety data, but please check with your local NOAA/NWS (National Oceanic and Atmospheric Administration/National Weather Service) for any updated safety information on severe weather.

Remember, storm chasing is for the pros and can be very dangerous. This book does NOT recommend chasing tornadoes, thunderstorms, or dust devils.

The author or Eakin Press shall not be responsible for loss or damage from the use of the severe weather information provided in this book.

Acknowledgments

My appreciation goes to Houston television weather anchor Robert Smith for his excellent answers to my questions about tornadoes.

Also I want to thank meteorologist Mike Kay for sharing his fascinating insights into storm chasing.

Thanks also to Hattie Krupala for her true story about how she survived a real Texas twister.

In addition, gratitude goes to the National Oceanic and Atmospheric Administration/National Weather Service for the tornado safety information in Chapter Five, which was taken from their *Watch Out ... Storms Ahead! Owlie Skywarn's Weather Book*.

Many thanks also to the Division of Emergency Management at the Texas Department of Public Safety for the use of their photographs.

Table of Contents

A Whirling Intro
(From the Author)

I grew up in Tornado Alley. Maybe that's why I've always been interested in tornadoes.

As a child, I remember stormy nights spent in our cellar. It smelled of squashed stickbugs and musty everything. But it proved a safe place during the wild winds of spring in Oklahoma. Down underground we listened to much weather madness. I always imagined the swirling death of a tornado would suck us all up. But it never came.

A few miles away, though, a tornado did come. It rammed into a little cafe. They rebuilt. Then another tornado walloped it. And they rebuilt again. We definitely lived in the heart of Tornado Alley.

As I said, I have an interest in tornadoes. But I'm not alone. Just about everybody I know has some fascination with these strange acts of nature. Why is that? I think partly because they are a bit of a mystery to us. People who study the weather still do not fully understand how they work.

Tornadoes are such curious creatures. They can pull up massive trees by their roots. And then toss them like pencils. Or create deadly missiles out of the rubble. A twister can tear off half of a house while leaving a teapot in the kitchen untouched.

Twisters strike us with wonder with their eerie shapes and vanishing acts. They can even be transparent until they pick up dust and debris. Some tornadoes can dip and curl gracefully in the middle of nowhere. Or they can come like cruel, dark cannons and make a town look like it had gone through a war. Tornadoes are enemies to man. And yet some say there is a beauty to them. Anyway you see them, they demand our attention!

In this book, *Texas Twisters*, the two characters, Kurt and Jessy, will let us explore the mystery of tornadoes with them. These two students are assigned to write a school research paper together on tornadoes in Texas. What they thought would be a boring school project turns into a real Texas-sized adventure for them.

After Kurt and Jessy interview a storm chaser, a TV weatherman, and a tornado survivor, they decide research can be "blow your hair back" fun. Then comes the "Sky Monster." Kurt and Jessy are faced with a real tornado while biking to the local "Dust Field." They both have to use what they've learned to survive this deadly twister.

Chapter 1

I'd Rather Eat Broccoli Pudding!

Kurt's mind screamed, "Please. Noooo!" He thought if he pretended it wasn't happening, maybe it would disappear. It was like a terrible dream, only he was awake.

Here he was in science class hearing the teacher assign him a big research paper on tornadoes. And even worse, the teacher made Oh No Jessy his research partner.

Oh No Jessy was a new kid in school, and all his friends said she was a monster. They called her Oh No Jessy because that's what everybody said when they saw her coming. "OH NO!" They said she was so mean she ate forks for breakfast.

This couldn't be happening to him. His life was over. And yes, it was worse than eating a mountain of broccoli pudding!

Maybe he could join the circus and become a fire-eating, lion-taming clown. That's the way he felt right now. Like a clown. And he never felt that way. He was too popular to feel like a clown.

Yes, he would have to do the research paper. And when it was all over, he would give himself something really great. But what if his only reward ended up being a black eye from you know who?

The school bell clanged, making Kurt jump in his seat. School finally ended for the day. After some ribbing from his friends about Oh No Jessy, Kurt plodded homeward.

"Hey, Kurt. Wait up!" somebody yelled from behind. It was Oh No Jessy! She was stalking him.

Kurt cringed. He was afraid to say "Hi." He thought it might set her off.

"Listen. We have to get our project started soon, because I have to go somewhere with my parents for a while. So, could we get started today?" Jessy asked.

Kurt answered, "Well ... OK. I guess."

"Maybe we could meet at the library today at four o'clock. OK?"

Kurt started to say no, but then he thought the sooner he got on with this mess the sooner he'd get out of it. "Yeah, I guess that's OK."

Just then several sparrows flew near their heads, swooping and chattering. Jessy exclaimed, "Look at the *boirds*."

Kurt rolled his eyes. "You mean, the *birds*?"

Jessy didn't smile. "Sorry. That's the way they say it where *I* come from." She hurried away, tossing her red hair. Suddenly she turned and hollered back, "You'd better be at the library."

Kurt picked up a pine cone. One of the spikes pricked his finger, and he winced. That's the way this project felt, he thought. Feeling sorry for himself, he kicked the pine cone all the way home.

Later at the library, Kurt saw Jessy coming up the walk. "You're the one late," Kurt said.

"Whatever," Jessy responded. "I know you don't really want to do this research with me. So we'll just hurry up and get it over with. Then you won't have to be with me. OK?"

"That's fine with me," replied Kurt.

"I don't know much about tornadoes," Jessy said. "And I don't know anything about TEXAS tornadoes."

Kurt remarked, "You don't know anything about tornadoes because you're from NEW YORK."

Jessy frowned. "What's wrong with being from New York?"

Kurt turned his lips up, pretending to smile. "Not a thing. Come on. Let's look through these books on weather and tornadoes."

Jessy flipped through some pages and saw a photo of a gigantic tornado. "Ohhhh. Look at this. This tornado is so spooky. And it's headed for this town. I'll bet it really did a lot of damage." Jessy almost shouted, "Hey! I've got an idea."

Some people in the library went, "Shhhhhh!"

"Listen," Jessy said, "the teacher told us we could interview people for our paper. How about we talk to some people about tornadoes?"

Kurt smoothed back his curly hair and groaned. "Like who?"

"I don't know. Like a TV weatherman or maybe talk to some people who've seen a tornado. That would be wild."

Kurt sighed. "I don't know. Maybe. Where are we going to find people who lived through a tornado?

Wait a minute. Somebody said this library had been hit by a tornado a long time ago."

"Really? And I heard about some people in the news who actually chase tornadoes. Maybe somebody at the TV station would know," Jessy suggested. Kurt said, "OK. We need to divide up the work here. Why don't you try to interview someone who chases tornadoes and then talk to the librarian about the tornado that hit here."

"And what are you going to do?" Jessy grumbled.

Kurt thought. "I'll interview a TV weatherman and collect some tornado safety information."

"Well, I guess that sounds sort of fair," Jessy said.

Kurt stared at Jessy while she was reading. She seemed angry some of the time, but she didn't really seem like a monster. And she hadn't even punched him once. But then ... tomorrow was another day.

Later with a load of books, Kurt sped toward home on his bike. He glanced over at "The Dirt Field," as everybody called it. There in the middle spun a dust devil.

"Double wow," Kurt whispered. It looked like a tiny tornado. It whirled upward, slinging dirt higher and higher. He'd seen them many times, but never this close. It headed right for him.

Before he had time to think of what to do next, the tiny funnel engulfed him. The wind whipped him hard. Dust bit into his face. He wobbled on his bike, nearly falling. Kurt cried out, his eyes burning from the bits of dirt.

Suddenly, stillness came. He slammed his brakes, rubbed his eyes, and gazed upward. He saw a cloudless sky above him. "I'm in the eye of a real dust devil," he hollered.

Chapter 2

Do People Really Chase Tornadoes?

All at once the other side of the dust devil whooshed against him. More dust and more wobbling. Then the wind eddy freed him.

Kurt just couldn't stop saying, "Double wow." He popped a wheely on his bike and sped home, charged with excitement about dust devils and tornadoes. And, well, maybe this research stuff wasn't as bad as he thought.

Three days later, Jessy bragged to Kurt, "Guess what I have?"

Kurt replied, "A bad cold? You better not get to close to me."

"No, goofy," said Jessy. "I talked to a real Texas storm chaser. He really chases tornadoes. Anyway his name is Mike Kay. He told me he's also a meteorologist."

"How did you do all that so fast?" Kurt asked.

"I don't know. He was real nice to talk to. He answered my questions on a tape recorder. Then I typed it all out. It was fun." Then Jessy asked, "Well, what have *you* done?"

Kurt tried to sound important, "Well, a dust devil hit me while I was on my bike. It felt crazy wild."

"Well, *you're* certainly crazy wild," Jessy replied. "You know, you'd better get with it. I'm going to be finished soon."

"OK, OK. Well, let's see what you have there," Kurt said.

Jessy handed her papers to Kurt. He glanced over it. "You mean he's seen twenty-five tornadoes? This is great. How did you know what questions to ask him?"

"I read through some books for ideas," Jessy replied.

"And look at all these pictures of tornadoes! They're super scary."

Jessy answered, "I got them from the Texas Department of Public Safety. It's really good stuff. You can look at all of it if you want to."

Kurt barely heard her. He'd already started reading Mike's true tales about storm chasing.

My name is Mike Kay, and I have been chasing tornadoes for about six years. My first storm chase was in the late spring of 1991. I have seen about twenty-five tornadoes since then.

I'm not really called a tornado chaser, though. A better term is storm chaser. I think everyone who storm chases hopes to see a tornado. But we see more thunderstorms than tornadoes. So storm chaser is a more accurate term.

I have always been interested in tornadoes. I grew up on the east coast. Tornadoes are not as common there. I believe my early interest was in thunderstorms in general.

I became a meteorologist because weather affects everyone. And because it is challenging to predict. I also feel weather is something everyone likes and appreciates.

I do love to hunt down tornadoes. I search for them because of their beauty. There is something very amazing in watching a tornado develop from a thunderstorm. The beauty of the atmosphere is another reason I storm chase. Every thunderstorm is unique. So is every tornado. This makes each storm special and memorable.

I chase storms for the excitement too. For instance, it is thrilling to see grapefruit sized hailstones come from a huge thunderstorm.

Another reason I chase thunderstorms is for the education. We hope to better understand how tornadoes form. This process is not yet very well understood. If we learn how they form, then warnings can be given earlier. We hope fewer people will get hurt this way.

Also, I learn more about how the atmosphere works. I can then apply these thoughts to computer models of thunderstorms. We use these computer models to understand what happens with real thunderstorms.

I chase a storm by car. I do not need a special vehicle. But it is important to have a vehicle that is dependable and roadworthy.

And I do not go by myself. This is for safety reasons. It can be very unsafe to be driving around a storm while making road choices. Plus, I have to watch the storm.

I usually chase with one other person. He is my chase partner. We've been chasing together since 1991. He's also a meteorologist. However, sometimes three or four of us will chase together in one vehicle.

We do most of our chasing in the Texas Panhandle. However, tornadoes happen in all parts of Texas. The Texas Panhandle has good visibility. It also has good roads and very good storms. Spring is when tornadoes most often occur. However, tornadoes occur year round. So we always have to keep ourselves ready to chase anytime of the year.

First, we make a forecast of where we think conditions are best for tornadoes. Then we spend many hours driving to that area.

Sometimes we can call other storm chasers who have information. We can ask them where the storms are.

Once there, we need to go to the right part of the thunderstorm. We then move as best we can along the storm. We watch for signs that a tornado might be developing. Finally, if everything is right, we might see a tornado.

The tornado will generally move in the same direction as the storm. It will also usually go the same speed. If we know how the thunderstorm is moving, we can use a road map to figure out how to move along with the tornado.

We stay on the roads. We do not drive on other people's property. And we try to keep a safe distance from the tornado.

If I know I am in a safe position, it is very exciting to see a tornado. If I am not in a safe location, then I spend my energy trying not to get hurt.

The closest I've ever gotten to a tornado was within one-half of a mile. Many people have said that tornadoes sound like a train coming. But so far I have not heard any strange sounds made by the tornadoes.

Tornadoes come in different shapes and sizes. I have seen skinny ones. These can be graceful and pretty. I have also seen tornadoes that were a mile wide. These can be wild and dark. They can also be full of dirt and debris.

To see a tornado is very exciting. It is a breathtaking sight ... to see it form and watch it grow. Then to see it slowly go away. This process can be very beautiful.

The oddest thing I've ever seen was a tornado pulling up the pavement on the road it crossed. Then the pavement was thrown far away into a field. I saw this happen with two different tornadoes.

I've seen some scary things too. One time we were following a storm after dark. We picked up some instruments which made some measurements of the storm. Suddenly another storm developed. It started moving toward us. This new storm caught us by surprise. The wind and rain blew hard. We could barely see.

All at once the winds shifted direction. This meant there was an area of rotation just above us. This was the beginning of a tornado. Fortunately, it passed over us.

After we drove away we found large limbs broken off trees. This was less than one-eighth of a mile from where we were. So we had been close to some real danger.

We are not the only ones who chase storms in Texas. The number has grown in the last several years. This is because more and more people are hearing about storm chasers. And it is becoming popular.

Many people come from other states. They come here in the spring just to chase storms. These people will often travel all over the central United States in search of tornadoes.

The whole process of storm chasing can be fulfilling when it succeeds. But storm chasing is also hard and tiring. It is not as glamorous as some believe. People do not realize how many hours and hours of driving it takes. On many chases you see nothing. In the spring of 1996 I drove 3,600 miles in six days. I went with my chase partner on the trip. We drove over parts of Texas, Oklahoma, Kansas, Nebraska, Colorado, and New Mexico. We saw only one tornado in Nebraska during this whole time. And that tornado lasted only five minutes!

There is no school to learn how to chase tornadoes. Although, there are schools to learn about the weather. I have tried to learn as much as I can about severe thunderstorms. This knowledge is valuable to me. I use it for my education, my job, and to chase storms more safely.

Keep in mind thunderstorms and especially tornadoes are VERY dangerous. If you are properly trained then the danger is not as great. But NOT just anybody should chase storms. Even to the trained eye it is not always easy to understand what you are seeing around thunderstorms. An untrained person can get into some serious danger. A person can be killed trying to chase a storm or a tornado. They can even be killed from the driving hazards, which can come from chasing. So, storm chasing is definitely NOT for people who are untrained.

Kurt's eyes widened. "Boy, I didn't know tornadoes were so spooky and interesting. This is great."

Jessy beamed. "Yeah, twisters are fun to learn about. Even if they are TEXAS Twisters."

Kurt noticed Jessy actually had an ordinary grin on her face. And it wasn't 'cause she was about to slug him or anything. Kurt began to wonder why his friends had been so hard on Jessy. She didn't seem too terrible.

Three more days later and it was Kurt's turn to tease Jessy at school. "Guess what I have?"

Jessy kidded back, "A bad hair day?"

"No. I got an interview with a TV weatherman. His name is Robert Smith and he works for a television station. He's also their chief meteorologist. How about that?" Kurt asked.

Jessy said, "OK, Mr. Smarty. Let's have a peek at your interview."

Chapter 3

Tornadoes Can Be Deadly

Kurt handed over his papers.

Jessy said, "That's wild. You've got it set up like a question and answer thing. It's fun to read that way. Let me just have a look here." Jessy buried her face in the papers and began to read.

QUESTION: What is a tornado?

ANSWER: A violently rotating column of air in contact with the ground.

QUESTION: Have you ever seen a real tornado?

ANSWER: Yes. I've seen a waterspout.

QUESTION: What is a waterspout?

ANSWER: It is similar to a tornado, but it forms over

the water. They are usually not as strong as a land based tornado. But they can overturn boats out on the water. Waterspouts form in somewhat the same way as a tornado, and they have a funnel.

QUESTION: How did you feel when you saw it?

ANSWER: I was on the beach for some enjoyment. It started to cloud up and rain. Then a waterspout formed. It ruined the day. But as a meteorologist, I was excited to see one. It started to move toward land where I was. But then it went back up into the clouds.

QUESTION: Do we get a lot of waterspouts in Texas?

ANSWER: Yes. We do get a lot of waterspouts out over the coastal waters of Texas.

QUESTION: Is the word "twister" another name for a tornado?

ANSWER: Yes. But "twister" is more of a slang term. Tornado is the term used more in meteorology.

QUESTION: What is a dust devil?

ANSWER: A dust devil is much smaller than a tornado, and does not have all the same atmospheric ingredients. Basically, dust devils are a turning and twisting of the wind over open fields. You can see the dust swirling in them.

QUESTION: What is the wind speed of most tornadoes?

ANSWER: A small tornado can have winds from

around 75 to 100 miles per hour. A major tornado has winds more than 300 miles per hour. In fact, no one knows how strong the winds can get. Some have said the winds may be from 300 to 500 miles per hour.

QUESTION: Why don't we know how fast the winds are?

ANSWER: Because no instrument has survived the tornado. Although, with new technology, gauging the wind speeds is getting more and more accurate.

QUESTION: How long do tornadoes usually last?

ANSWER: Most tornadoes don't last long at all. Sometimes they last only minutes. But some have stayed on the ground for hours. They can even travel across states.

QUESTION: What part of Texas gets the most tornadoes?

ANSWER: Our part of Tornado Alley is in North Central Texas, from around Wichita Falls going north. But there's really no sharp line for it. It's not like you're just driving along and suddenly you're in Tornado Alley. It's just the general area.

QUESTION: What county has the most tornadoes in Texas?

ANSWER: The county we live in—Harris County. It often has more reported tornadoes than any county in the United States. And we are not even in Tornado Alley. But most of the tornadoes in Harris County are small tornadoes. In Tornado Alley they get really big ones.

QUESTION: What do the clouds look like, right before a tornado forms?

ANSWER: The clouds will darken and begin to lower. And there will be one part of the cloud base that will drop down lower than the rest of the cloud base. This is called the "wall cloud." It is a very distinct lowering of a section of the cloud in the sky. That "wall cloud" may start turning. Then the tornado will form.

QUESTION: What type of clouds form tornadoes?

ANSWER: Cumulonimbus clouds.

QUESTION: Does a green sky mean a tornado is coming?

ANSWER: A green sky can mean a tornado is coming, but not always. Sometimes it means the sky is packed with a lot of hail. And many times large hail is associated with tornadoes.

QUESTION: How wide can a tornado get?

ANSWER: Most tornadoes are just a few hundred yards wide. But some of the big tornadoes can be over a mile wide.

QUESTION: What do you think makes the tornado?

ANSWER: Tornadoes normally occur where there is

a clash of air masses. The cold air meets the warm air. That is why Texas is such a breeding ground for tornadoes. We have the warm, moist air coming in from the Gulf of Mexico. And it clashes with the cooler air coming in from the north.

QUESTION: Is there a tornado season?

ANSWER: There is no official tornado season like hurricane season (the first day of June to the last of November is hurricane season). But spring is typically when we get the most tornadoes. Because we are getting the change of seasons. We still have the cold air coming down from the north. But we're starting to see the transition where we have warm air coming up from the Gulf. That is why we have more tornadoes in the spring.

QUESTION: What month do we get the most tornadoes?

ANSWER: Generally May.

QUESTION: Can tornadoes happen in all parts of the world?

ANSWER: Yes, in most parts of the world. But no place do they occur more often than in the United States and right in Tornado Alley.

QUESTION: Why are tornadoes different colors?

ANSWER: It depends on the terrain they are moving over. If they are moving over water then they will have a clearer look to them. If they are moving over a farm field, then it will look dark. It can also depend upon whether there is a lot of hail associated with it, or a lot of moisture.

QUESTION: Why do tornadoes come in different shapes?

ANSWER: Every storm is different. And the winds and the pressure may not be the same each time. It's like looking up at the clouds and seeing different formations. The wind is moving the clouds around differently every day.

QUESTION: Can you have tornadoes inside tornadoes?

ANSWER: Some of the big tornadoes have multiple vortices. The actual twisting rope you see may have several inside. They will look like one big tornado because of the dark massive cloud. But inside that cloud there may be several vortices turning.

QUESTION: Can you have separate tornadoes side by side?

ANSWER: Yes. Sometimes you can look at the horizon and see several separate tornadoes. And these are not part of the same tornado cloud. I have heard of six or seven tornadoes near each other at the same time.

QUESTION: What kind of damage can tornadoes do?

ANSWER: A small tornado can break small tree

trunks, knock over light objects, and remove shingles from your roof. The stronger tornadoes can overturn trains and trucks. They can level homes so there is nothing left but the concrete slab.

QUESTION: Besides Texas, what are the other states in Tornado Alley?

ANSWER: Mostly Oklahoma, Kansas, and Nebraska, but much of the plains and other states east of the Rockies have tornadoes. Few tornadoes occur west of the Rockies.

QUESTION: Is it true Texas gets the most tornadoes?

ANSWER: Yes, on average, Texas does. We have the conditions suitable for tornadoes here in Texas. But it is also because we have such a large state. We have about 120 tornadoes per year. Oklahoma has under 100 tornadoes per year. But Oklahoma often has the most tornadoes per square mile than any other state.

QUESTION: Can any part of Texas get a tornado?

ANSWER: Probably yes. But far West Texas gets very few, because the air is very dry. And there are few down along the Rio Grande where there is very little moisture.

QUESTION: Can tornadoes pass over mountains, hills, and canyons?

ANSWER: Yes, but where they form in the plains, there aren't any mountains.

QUESTION: What was one of the worst tornadoes in Texas history?

ANSWER: One of the worst was the Wichita Falls tornado of 1979. It was a massive storm and killed and injured many people. It also did a lot of damage.

QUESTION: What are two of the most useful ways to spot tornadoes?

ANSWER: Now Doppler radar is very useful. Conventional radar shows basically where it is raining. But Doppler can actually look at the wind field and show us the way the wind is moving. Doppler radar can give meteorologists several minutes of lead time because we can look at the contrasting wind directions the Doppler radar is displaying. Also, people who are trained storm spotters are very useful in spotting tornadoes.

QUESTION: Can you see tornadoes from space?

ANSWER: You can see hurricanes from space. But it depends on how high up in space you're talking about. You can see the storm clouds that are producing the tornadoes. But since the tornadoes are on the underside of the storm clouds, you probably wouldn't see them.

QUESTION: Can hurricanes make tornadoes?

ANSWER: Well, tornadoes very frequently are offshoots of, or are born from, hurricanes.

QUESTION: Does a tornado spin around clockwise or counterclockwise?

ANSWER: Usually counterclockwise.

QUESTION: Which direction does a tornado travel?

ANSWER: Most tornadoes move from the southwest to the northeast. Maybe 80 percent or more do that.

QUESTION: Are there strength levels to tornadoes?

ANSWER: Yes. The strength level of tornadoes is on a scale of 0 to 5. It is often referred to as the Fujita Scale. F0 is the smallest and F5 is a major tornado.

QUESTION: Has Texas ever had an F5 tornado?

ANSWER: Yes, it's probably had many over the years.

QUESTION: What are some of the strange things tornadoes can do?

ANSWER: Tornadoes can take a piece of straw and put it through a telephone pole. They can destroy everything around the house, but leave the house intact. I've heard people have been picked up and transported by tornadoes. They are taken great distances and then later put down unharmed. Cars can get tossed around like matchboxes. A large tornado can pick up a car and take it into the atmosphere hundreds or thousands of feet—then it might be slung miles away.

QUESTION: What can a tornado sound like?

ANSWER: A common sound is a freight train. But

people have heard other noises like jet engines or a loud roar.

QUESTION: Can tornadoes cause fires?

ANSWER: Yes. If they hit electrical transformers and things like that.

QUESTION: Can a tornado happen in hail and rain?

ANSWER: Yes. But tornadoes sometimes form in the rain-free base of the storm cloud. But near them you can see the rain and the hail. Often times you can see a green colored sky. That usually means a cloud is packed with hail.

QUESTION: Can a tornado happen when it is snowing?

ANSWER: That is highly unlikely. But you can have thunder snow showers. That is where you have thundering and lightning while it is snowing.

QUESTION: Can a tornado happen while the sun is shining?

ANSWER: It can happen while the sun is shining in some parts of the sky. But the tornado must form in a thunderstorm cloud. So there couldn't be sun shining right there.

QUESTION: Do people really chase tornadoes?

ANSWER: Yes.

QUESTION: Why do they do that?

ANSWER: Partly for the excitement. And some of it is for research purposes.

QUESTION: What do storm chasers learn from this activity?

ANSWER: They are trying to get a more accurate measurement of the wind speeds. They are trying to learn more about how tornadoes develop.

QUESTION: What is their main goal?

ANSWER: Probably to learn how to predict the tornadoes' beginnings. We can't stop the tornadoes from forming. So we need a better understanding about what causes them to form. Because even with all the theories, there are still a lot of unanswered questions.

QUESTION: Would this information give people more time to get to safety?

ANSWER: Yes. That is my understanding of the purpose. And also maybe to better plan the construction of buildings to withstand the tornadoes.

QUESTION: Do you think scientists will someday be able to stop tornadoes?

ANSWER: Perhaps. But I don't think so.

QUESTION: What time of day do most tornadoes form?

ANSWER: Most tornadoes occur in the late afternoon and early evening hours.

QUESTION: Why is that?

ANSWER: Mainly because of the afternoon heating. The sun is an important part of getting the earth cooked up, explosive, and ready for tornadoes.

QUESTION: Do you think we get more tornadoes now than years ago?

ANSWER: I don't think it's any more or any less now. But the number of tornadoes does vary from year to year. Some years we have a very active year. And some years there are less. Texas has about 120 tornadoes per year. I've seen that number go down to the eighties or nineties. Then it might go back up the next year to one hundred and something.

QUESTION: Did you always want to be a weatherman?

ANSWER: No. I got into this business by accident. But once I got into it I went into high gear. I learned everything I could possibly learn in the business. Now I give speeches to schools, groups, and other organizations. And I train weathercasters also.

QUESTION: What type of weather in Texas is the most interesting to you?

ANSWER: The tornado is the most awesome thing to

study. Considering its size, there is nothing on earth that can equal it.

Jessy read all of Kurt's research paper. Then she slammed it down on the desk.

"What? You hate it?" Kurt asked.

"No, it's so good, I'm mad," answered Jessy. Then her blue eyes smiled again.

Kurt decided right then Jessy definitely didn't look ugly when she smiled like that.

A few days later at school Jessy dropped some papers in front of Kurt. He knew what it was ... the tornado survivor interview with a librarian named Miss Hatti. Yes! She got it. He could tell it was going to be terrific. Immediately, he started to read Miss Hatti's true story.

Chapter 4

I Survived a Tornado!

1992. I could never forget it. That year I survived a tornado.

I had gone out to lunch that Saturday before Thanksgiving. The sun shone warm and bright. I thought, "What a beautiful day!"

Then I drove back to the library where I work. Bustling activity kept us from paying any attention to the weather. Then all at once we lost power in the library. I peered out the window to see the weather. I noticed the sky glowed an eerie green. And the wind blew hard, whipping the trees around. I felt then something was very wrong outside.

Suddenly someone in the library yelled, "There's a tornado. Take cover!"

Some of the people crawled under the tables. Other people crouched down.

It all happened so quickly. The next thing we knew a tornado tore off the roof of our library building. Rocks from the top of the building pelted my head. I thought, "I wonder if I will survive this!"

I didn't hear a roar from the tornado, but the wind slammed the heavy glass doors open in front of the library. You could feel the force of it.

Some of the children screamed.

A heavy air conditioner unit on top of our library crashed through the building as the roof came off. It landed behind us in the hallway. Then another air conditioner unit thundered down into the workroom.

But just as quickly as the tornado dipped down and took our roof off, it disappeared. The inside of the library gave us a strange sight. The top of the building had vanished. Rain fell into the library. It rained on the books and computers and tables. I looked around. An enormous mess waited for someone to clean up, but not now.

The sheriff's department hurried over. They smelled natural gas in the library. They wanted everyone out of the building quickly, fearing something would happen. They thought the building might explode.

We quickly crossed the street to the courthouse where we took shelter. As I left the building, shock came to me as I discovered the destruction done to the cars by the tornado. The glass on the windshields had been blown in and shattered. The winds had bashed the cars into each other like toys.

The tornado had also done a lot of damage to a nearby building. It had skipped over the highway and dropped down with violence again, destroying some homes.

We felt fortunate in the library. There were no deaths. I'm very grateful for that.

As I look back on what happened to me, I guess I wasn't that scared, because I didn't have *time* to get scared. It all happened so quickly. I was just glad to be alive.

But sometime after that I worried when I saw a thunderstorm. I wondered, "Is it going to happen all over again? I don't want to go through that again!"

Now that years have passed, I don't feel that same way about storms. But I will always take a tornado watches and warnings seriously. Everyone should!

Kurt read the last line. Jessy sat down at the table.

She asked, "It's good, isn't it?"

"It's so good, it scared me," answered Kurt. "Yes, we are s-o-o-o good. And here is my stuff." Kurt handed over his latest part of the research paper.

"Is this your tornado safety stuff?" asked Jessy.

"Yep. It's good information from the NOAA/NWS. The NOAA stands for the National Oceanic and Atmospheric Administration and the NWS stands for the National Weather Service."

Jessy said, "That sounds important. So what are you supposed to do if there's a tornado coming?"

Chapter 5

Tornado Safety Tips

Kurt shrugged his shoulders. "I don't know. I just got it in the mail. Let's read it and find out."

Jessy and Kurt leaned in to read.

TORNADO

If you ever see a big black cloud with a funnel-like extension beneath it, watch out. It could be a tornado.

A tornado looks like a funnel with the fat part at the top. Inside, its winds may be swirling around at 300 miles an hour. If it goes through a town, the tornado could flatten houses and buildings, lift up cars and trucks, and shatter mobile homes into splinters. Sometimes the path is narrow, but everything in the path is wrecked. But you don't always see the funnel. It may be raining too hard. Or the tornado may come at night. Listen for the tornado's roar. Some people say it sounds like a thousand trains.

TORNADO WATCH

The Weather Service forecasts that a tornado may develop later. The sky may be blue at the time you hear the watch. Don't be fooled. Listen to the radio for the latest news.

TORNADO WARNING

A tornado has been sighted. It may move toward you. Dark clouds boil in the sky.

There may be thunder and lightning and heavy rain. And there may be hail. When you see large hail, you may be close to a tornado. Seek shelter.

Power may go off. Funnels reach down from the black clouds.

WHAT TO DO

In your house ...

- When you hear the *tornado watch*, keep your eye on the sky for signs of a possible tornado and listen to the radio for the latest advice from the National Weather Service. When you hear the *warning*, act to protect yourself.
- Get away from windows. They may shatter, and glass may go flying.
- Go to the basement. Get under a heavy workbench or the stairs.
- If there is no basement, go to an inside closet, bathroom, or hallway on the lowest level of the house.
- Get under a mattress. Protect your head.
- If you live in a mobile home, get out. Even if it's tied down, a mobile home can be shattered by a tornado. The whole thing can be lifted up and dropped. Get out and into a safer place. Some mobile home areas have storm

shelters. If you can't get to a shelter, lie in a ditch and cover your head with your hands.

Downtown or in a shopping mall ...
+ Get off the street.
+ Go into a building, stay away from windows and doors.

Outside ...
+ Get out of a car and inside a house or building.
+ Don't try to outrun a tornado in a car. Tornadoes can pick up a car and throw it through the air.
+ If you're caught outside, lie in a ditch. Or crouch near a strong building.
+ Cover your head with your hands.
+ Follow directions.
+ Go to an inside hall on the lowest floor.
+ Crouch near the wall. Bend over with your hands on the back of your head.
+ Keep away from glass and stay out of big rooms like the gym, cafeteria, or auditorium.
+ Keep a battery radio on. Listen for news about the tornado.

IN YOUR SCHOOL

In general ...
+ And remember, when there's a tornado there can be a lot of lightning.
+ Stay away from anything that uses electricity.
+ Stay away from anything metal—faucets, radiators, sinks, and tubs.

Tornadoes are scary.
They pack a lot of energy;
enough to blow down a whole town.
But you can live through a tornado.
Don't panic. Be smart, know what to do, and **do it.**

Jessy said, "I'm sure glad I read that."

"Yeah, the teacher is going to love it. We'll slam-dunk an 'A' easy," Kurt added.

Suddenly, Jessy thought she heard something. Something like distant thunder. But she couldn't tell for sure. Jessy remarked, "Texas sure is different from New York. Where I come from people talk more about blizzards than tornadoes."

"Oh, yeah? Well, parts of Texas can get some mean winter storms too. So there!" Kurt teased.

Jessy kidded back, "And you sure do meet the strangest friends here."

Did she say friend? Kurt wondered. Couldn't be. Could it?

"Hey, I have an idea," Jessy said. "Why don't we show the class how to make a tornado in a jar full of water. Remember, the teacher said we could use props." Kurt blurted, "Yeah! That's good. We'll take a big glass jar, fill it with water, and stir it super fast with a stick. It'll look like the real thing. Neat idea." Jessy beamed with pride.

Later after school, Kurt saw Jessy riding her bike home. "Hey, wait up," he called out.

Jessy just kept riding.

Kurt wondered why she didn't stop. He hollered again, "Hey, Jessy. Wait up, OK?"

Suddenly Jessy peered back. She stopped and waved at Kurt.

Within a moment Kurt had caught up with her on his bike. He asked, "Hey, didn't you hear me hollering?"

"Not really. The wind is blowing so hard, I'm having trouble hearing," Jessy said.

Kurt glanced around. Funny, he hadn't even noticed. She was right. The breeze had really picked up. The tall pines bowed and creaked in the gusts of wind. Like a chilling fever, cool and warm air swirled around him. "Boy, the wind sure is in a bad mood. Look at the tops of those trees."

Jessy squinted, staring upward. "That's kind of creepy. They sound like they're going to snap and crash down on our heads."

Kurt asked, "Hey, want to go watch for dust devils? Sometimes when I ride over by The Dirt Field, I see one."

"Sure, but just because I want to see one, doesn't mean it's going to be there. It's not like ordering up fries and a Coke," Jessy replied.

But before Kurt could agree, Jessy said, "Sure, why not? Let's go."

They both raced to The Dirt Field. They screeched to a halt and sat. They waited and waited, watching for the possible surprise of a tiny whirlwind. Soon the Texas summer heat seared them like a blowtorch. Kurt's forehead dripped with sweat, little beads chasing down his cheeks.

Finally Jessy groaned, "Hey, I don't want to watch for dust devils anyway. We might get knocked down by one and end up breaking something ... like our heads."

Kurt said, "Did you hear something? It sounded like thunder." Kurt glanced back. Just behind them the clouds radiated a spooky green. "Don't look now, but there's a green-eyed monster behind us."

Chapter 6

The Sky Monster

Jessy grinned, "Yeah, right. And there's a little elf in your pocket too." Jessy looked behind her though, just in case. She gasped. "When did *that* happen? It was a pretty day a little while ago!"

"I know. The sky looks like it's been gorging on avocados," Kurt said.

"Wait a minute. In our interviews, didn't they say a green sky could come before a tornado?" Jessy asked.

Kurt laughed. "We've been spending too much time writing about tornadoes. Now we're thinking they're creeping up on us. It's like when you watch a scary movie; you always have to keep peeking over your shoulder for a day or two. This is just the same. A green sky doesn't *always* mean a tornado. Right?"

"Yeah, I guess so," Jessy agreed. "Kind of like being alive doesn't *always* mean you'll be happy."

"What does that mean?"

"Just what I said," Jessy replied. "Nobody promised me things would be wonderful. And it's a good thing they didn't. 'Cause they would have been lying."

"I still don't understand."

"I don't understand either." Jessy locked eyes with Kurt. "It's my mom. She's sick."

Kurt didn't know what to say, so he just listened.

"My mom has cancer," Jessy said. "They don't know if she'll live. That's why I have to leave for a while with my parents. They're going to try some new treatment for it. They don't know if it'll work."

"That's bad. I mean your mom. I would hate it if my mom had that," Kurt said.

"Yeah. I hate it too." Jessy admitted, "It makes me angry sometimes."

"Is that why you hit people?" Kurt asked.

Jessy frowned. "I only did that once. I was defending myself from one of *your* friends."

Kurt suddenly felt rotten that his friends had treated her so badly. They had said so many mean things about her. She wasn't a monster at all. She wasn't OH NO JESSY. She was just Jessy. They had been wrong. He felt like a jerk for listening to them. Kurt said, "I'm sorry about all that. I guess they just don't know when to stop pestering people."

"I know the kids here don't like me too much," Jessy said. "I sound funny to them because of my New York accent. I dress funny. And then sometimes I'm angry about what's happening to my mom. So nobody really wants to be with me or sit

---

34

with me at lunch. And now, I don't even feel like being friends with me either."

Kurt wondered what that felt like. He had always had friends. And most of the time he felt like he belonged. Now he saw the other side. And he had been part of the wall that had kept her out.

"Listen," Kurt said. "I'm sorry. My friends decided they didn't like you, so that's it. That's the way they are. If they like you, you're in. And if they don't, well, they don't. We've all been kind of jerky to you."

"Yeah," Jessy replied. "OK." She wiped the tear from her face. "Thanks for saying that."

"Maybe," Kurt said, "we could try and ..." Kurt's voice trailed off as his eyes widened. "Double wow."

"What's the matter, Kurt? Are you all right?" Jessy followed Kurt's gaze. Massive white clouds boiled and glimmered with lightning. She whispered, "That's wild. Cumulonimbus clouds. The kind that can produce tornadoes!"

Before Kurt could answer, thunder exploded around them, making them jump.

Kurt exclaimed, "And look at that thing hanging down over there. It's a part of the cloud. It's lowering ... isn't it?"

"I think that's called a wall cloud," Jessy said, her fear building.

Kurt forced his voice to steady. "Look, there's a cone-shaped thing. I think it's a funnel cloud!"

"Now look. The funnel! It looks like it's touching the ground over there! That makes it a tornado. Right?" Jessy yelled.

They froze in awe at the sight. The writing

tornado snaked its way through their neighborhood. It looked like something coming alive from one of their books, haunting and deadly. But this one loomed real before them. And this one could kill.

The tornado darkened from debris. Possibly debris from their own homes, Kurt thought. Fear crawled up his spine. He shivered.

Suddenly torn from the trance, he realized they had to move fast. "We can't go home. It's too far. But there's a ditch out here. That's what we're supposed to do. Remember?"

Jessy, hollered, "Look. The tornado. It's leaving!"

Kurt watched. She was right. The body of the cloud seemed to yank up its dangling and corpse-like arm. Then the last of its ghostly fingers dissolved like smoke.

Kurt whispered, "If it's gone, why don't I feel better? Wait a minute. Didn't we read in a book tornadoes can pick up and then drop back down again? Does the air smell funny? It's my imagination, I guess."

Jessy said, "The wind *is* picking up again. Where is that ditch you were talking about?"

"It's a hole some kids dug for a hideout," Kurt said. "Come on. We'd better get in it . . . just in case."

Suddenly, lightning crackled to the ground. The jolt of fire blasted a lone tree, splitting it down the middle. Sparks sprayed the air like deadly fireworks.

Jessy screamed, "We're like lightning rods out here. We'd better hurry or we'll get struck too."

"Follow me. Run!" Kurt shouted.

Lightning struck again not far from the hideout. Its crashing brightness took their breath away. They kept running toward the hole. Something made Jessy glance back. She couldn't believe what she saw. "Kurt! The tornado! It's touched down behind us!"

Kurt looked back as he ran. The tornado churned and roared behind them.

Its blackened vortex raged against an orange sky. It seemed like a hideous Halloween nightmare—a violent monster without eyes.

They screamed in horror.

Kurt saw the lightning scorched tree sucked straight out of the ground. Suddenly a glass door hurled right in front of them. It crashed leaving a jagged edge sticking straight up. Terrified, they both leaped over the savage-looking shard of glass. Unhurt, they kept running.

Kurt yelled, "JUMP!" Then they tumbled down into the hole.

Something hard hit Jessy in the arm and she cried out. "Hail! Now there's hail."

Like stinging wasps, the hailstones pelted them without mercy. Jessy slipped. Kurt caught her before she fell down into the mud.

"Lean into the side of the hole!" Kurt hollered. "Maybe the hail will miss us."

They mashed themselves against the side. Mud coated their clothes and faces.

Curiosity overcame them, and they peered over the edge. Yards away, their bikes lifted off the ground and became part of the vortex. A rake flew straight over them, barely missing their heads.

They both heard a loud sound. The winds

churned and roared above them like a locomotive. They clasped their hands over their ears.

Jessy screamed long and hard, hoping it would drive the clawing fear away. "It's here! It will suck us up. I know it will. What do we do?"

Kurt yelled, "This *is* the best place. A ditch, remember? There's no time to go anywhere else."

Jessy hollered back, "You're right. They said not to panic. Let's think. Think. Flat. I thought somebody said if we get caught outside, we should *lie* in a ditch. And our hands should cover our heads!"

Quickly, they slammed themselves flat against the bottom of the muddy hole, covered their heads with their hands, and prayed like crazy.

In moments, the winds calmed. The sudden silence haunted the air with an eerie peace.

Jessy whispered, "Do you think we're in the eye? Do you think it's coming back?"

Kurt answered, "I don't know. Maybe. But we'd better just stay here for a minute."

Sunlight poured over them. This time it felt like a warm hug. They heard birds twittering again as if nothing but a breeze had ever passed over them.

Jessy chuckled. "If it's gone, then how come we're so scared to get up?"

Slowly, ever so slowly, they rose up from the mire. Looking over the edge, they both saw . . . nothing. Absolute nothing.

Kurt smiled at Jessy. "Guess what? It *is* gone. And we're still alive."

With the terror behind them, they got a good look at each other. They both dripped with mud.

Leaves clung to the goo, making them look like strange beasts coming out to forage.

They shot each other a wide grin.

Suddenly, Jessy daintily flicked some of the brown goo onto Kurt's head. He fired back with another wad of mud right on her cheek. They flung little chunks of mud at each other until their smiles burst into chuckles. Soon they roared with laughter, thinking how silly they looked, and how good it felt to be alive!

Then Kurt slipped and fell face down in the mud. They laughed some more until their sides ached.

Finally a shadow of concern covered Kurt's face. "My mom. I have to go and see if she's safe. Were your parents home?"

"No," answered Jessy. "They're at the hospital."

Kurt said, "My mom. She was there when it hit."

Jessy said, "Your mom knew what to do. Didn't she read all your safety stuff?"

"Yeah, I guess. But I left the house all mad this morning. She always says, 'I love you.' I didn't say it. I should have said it, but I was angry. I wouldn't want anything to happen to my mom."

Jessy put her arm on his shoulder, "I understand."

Then Kurt realized she really *did* understand.

Jessy said, "I hope she's all right."

"Me too," replied Kurt. "I guess we'd better get our bikes and find out."

"Our bikes are gone, remember?"

"That's right. Gone. It will take us a while to get home now," Kurt said.

They started to climb out of the hole. Slipping

and sliding, they grabbed onto tree roots to lift themselves out.

Kurt picked up a large piece of hail and rolled it around in his hands. "What a storm that was. We thought it was a joke. But it was real. We didn't take the clouds seriously."

Jessy reminded him, "Yeah, but once we knew we were in trouble, we tried to do the right things. And it saved our lives."

"I didn't realize how important all that safety stuff was about tornadoes . . . until now," Kurt admitted.

"You said it!" Jessy squinted. "What is *that* over there? It almost looks like our bikes."

Kurt let out a yelp. "It *is*. What do you know?"

They ran to their bikes.

"They're fine. I can't believe it. They told us that, remember? Sometimes tornadoes set things back down without a scratch," Jessy said.

Totally giddy, they rode around in fast circles.

"No one will believe us," Jessy sang out.

Kurt replied, "You're right. But then I don't care. I know *you* believe it. Even if only one friend believes me, that's enough."

Jessy couldn't believe that either. "Did you just call me friend? Are you sure that hail didn't shake your brain loose?"

"Nope. My brain is feeling totally together."

Jessy grinned all over the place.

She is almost pretty when she smiles like that, Kurt thought. Even if she *is* smeared with mud.

Jessy suggested. "Do you want me to go with you to see if your mom is OK?"

"I guess. But then you'd better get home too—to see if your house is still standing."

"My parents aren't there right now," replied Jessy. "And I'm more concerned about your mom than my house."

Kurt thought that seemed just like something a *real* friend would say. "OK. Thanks," he answered.

They rode like maniacs. The closer they got to Kurt's house the more worried he got. Finally, they turned the corner to his street.

They both just stared in disbelief. Three houses had been torn up badly and yet the others were not even missing a shingle.

"That's my house. Over there ... the two-story brick one. It seems to be OK. My mom must be OK!"

Debris littered the sidewalk. They stepped over fence boards, trees, and a broken birdbath. It seemed so strange to Kurt that a wind could do so much damage.

"Nobody seems to be around. I guess a lot of people are at work," Kurt said. He stepped on a board and heard a yelp. "What was that?"

They looked underneath and saw a terrier pup.

"Hi, boy. Don't be scared," Jessy said.

They both yanked on the board until it pulled loose. The little dog raced up the street scared, but glad to be free.

Kurt said, "He's headed home now. He should be all right." Moments later, Kurt banged on his front door.

Kurt's mother emerged, worried. "Oh, thank God, you're all right. I thought so many frightful things. Look at you. What happened? Were you in the storm?" Tears streaming, she hugged her son tightly.

Kurt hugged his mom back like he hadn't seen her in a year. "I love you, Mom."

"I love you too," his mom replied. "You know, I thought maybe you went to the library. I called there, and they said they hadn't seen you. Oh, I am so grateful you are all right. And your friend too."

"Mom, this is Jessy. We saw the tornado. It passed right over us. We were in the muddy hole at The Dirt Field."

"Oh, my," Kurt's mom said. "You were watching for dust devils, again. Right?"

Kurt looked a little sheepish. "Yeah. I was hoping Jessy could see one."

Kurt's mom kidded, "I think you were hoping too hard. You saw a lot more than a dust devil this time."

They all laughed together. It felt good, Kurt thought. He said, "I'm glad you're OK, Mom. I saw the tornado go over our houses, and I got scared. I thought that ..."

His mom hugged him again. "I know what you thought. I'm OK. Several of the neighbors got quite a bit of damage. But we'll all chip in and help them."

"Mom," Kurt asked, "is it OK if I go with Jessy right now? I want to make sure her house is OK."

"Sure. But be back before supper. I know you'll want to scrape some of that mud off."

Kurt said, "OK."

They were off again, and before too long they turned the corner to Jessy's street.

"This is it," Jessy said with relief.

The house was small, but neatly kept. Kurt noticed that not even a flower in the front yard had been pulled up by the storm.

"It's OK, too," Jessy said, thankfully. "I guess I'd better call my mom and dad to tell them I'm OK in case they heard about the storm here."

"That's good," Kurt answered. "I hope that your mom gets better. And, well, I'll see you at school tomorrow. We can sit together at lunch."

"Are you sure your friends won't mind?" Jessy asked.

Kurt got on his bike and replied, "If they do, they'll just have to find another table."

Jessy couldn't believe what she heard. "Really? You'd do that for me?"

Kurt started to ride away. He smiled back at her and said loudly, "I'd do it in a New York minute!!"

Conclusion

A Stirring Finish

Just in case you're curious about what happened to the research paper Kurt and Jessy worked on, it was a total success. Everyone was so amazed that the teacher called the local newspaper about her students' work and survival adventure. Kurt and Jessy were interviewed, and the story ended up on the front page.

And, of course, Kurt and Jessy became good friends.

A Little Glossary of Terms

CUMULONIMBUS CLOUDS—Big, fluffy clouds, usually producing thunderstorms, hailstorms, or heavy rains, and can produce tornadoes as well.

DOPPLER RADAR—A type of radar that can spot the possible beginnings of a tornado.

DUST DEVIL—A small whirlwind of swirling dust.

FUJITA SCALE—A scale from F0 to F5 that gauges the damage produced by a tornado.

FUNNEL CLOUD—Turning winds in a cone-like extension from a storm cloud.

METEOROLOGIST—A person who studies the science of weather.

METEOROLOGY—The study of weather.

STORM CHASER—A person who chases storms for research and/or enjoyment.

THUNDERSTORM—A moving, often violent storm of thunder, lightning, and rain which may also produce hail and tornadoes.

TORNADO—A funnel touching the ground with violent turning winds.

TORNADO ALLEY—The central states where there are the most tornadoes—primarily Texas, Oklahoma, Kansas, and Nebraska.

TRAINED STORM SPOTTERS—People who are trained to spot storms and tornadoes and report them to the National Weather Service.

TWISTER—Another term for tornado.

VORTEX—A whirling column of air.

VORTICES—More than one vortex.

WALL CLOUD—A lowering of part of a storm cloud, which could be the beginning of a tornado.

WATERSPOUT—A tornado that forms over the water.

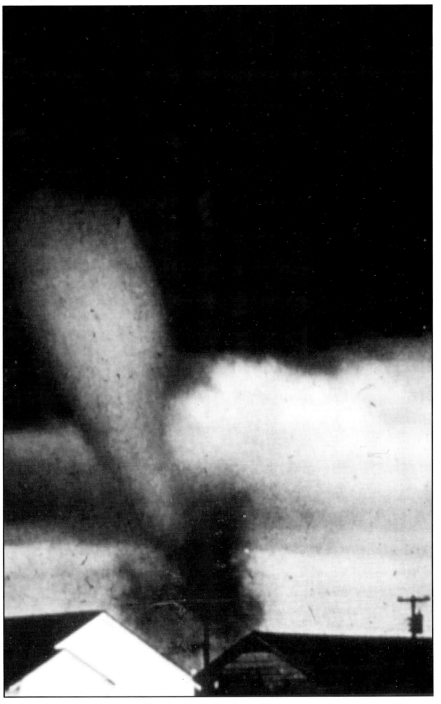

Tornado in Dallas, Texas
(Courtesy Division of Emergency Management,
Department of Public Safety)

Texas tornado
(Courtesy Division of Emergency Management,
Department of Public Safety)

Destruction from a tornado in Lubbock, Texas
(Courtesy Division of Emergency Management,
Department of Public Safety)

Tornado, Wichita Falls, Texas
(Courtesy Division of Emergency Management,
Department of Public Safety)

Leaves, limbs, and even bark were taken off by a tornado.
(Courtesy Division of Emergency Management,
Department of Public Safety)

Car and house disaster from a Texas tornado
(Courtesy Division of Emergency Management,
Department of Public Safety)

Tornado, Wichita Falls, Texas
(Courtesy Division of Emergency Management,
Department of Public Safety)

Tornado, Wichita Falls, Texas
(Courtesy Division of Emergency Management,
Department of Public Safety)

Destruction from a tornado in Sweetwater, Texas
(Courtesy Division of Emergency Management,
Department of Public Safety)

Train derailed by a tornado
(Courtesy Division of Emergency Management,
Department of Public Safety)

Tornado in Texas
(Courtesy Division of Emergency Management,
Department of Public Safety)

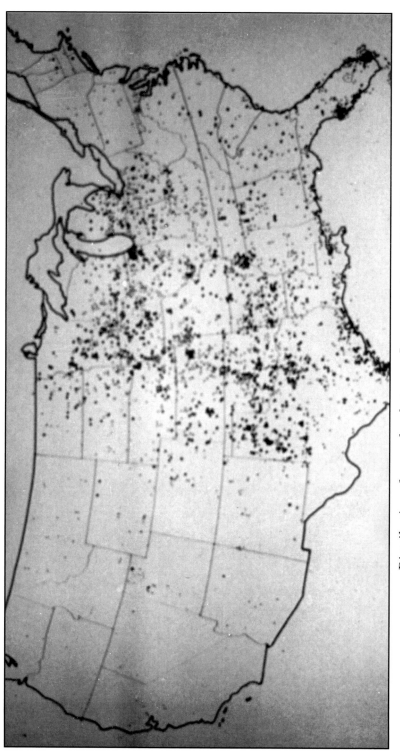

Distribution of severe local storms: January 1–August 31, 1968
(Courtesy Division of Emergency Management,
Department of Public Safety)

Tornado, Wichita Falls, Texas
(Courtesy Division of Emergency Management,
Department of Public Safety)

Car wrapped in a tree from a tornado
(Courtesy Division of Emergency Management,
Department of Public Safety)

Tornado in Wichita Falls, Texas, in 1979
(Courtesy Division of Emergency Management,
Department of Public Safety)

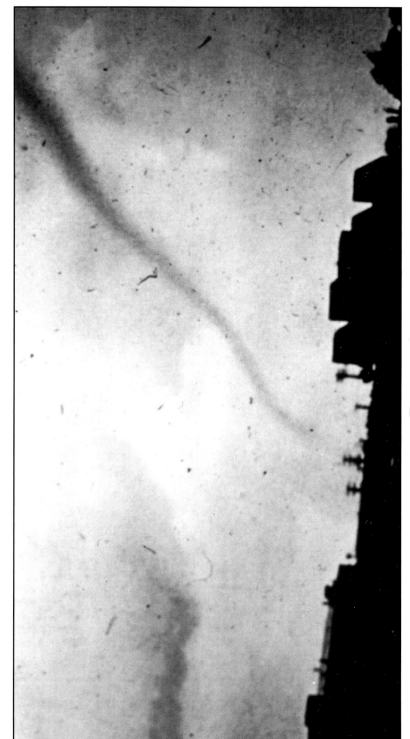

Texas tornado
(Courtesy Division of Emergency Management,
Department of Public Safety)